First U.S. edition 2006

First published by Walker Books Ltd.
87 Vauxhall Walk, London SE11 5HJ

Library of Congress Cataloging-in-Publication Data is available.

Library of Congress Catalog Card Number 2006042569

ISBN-10 0-7636-3121-3
ISBN-13 978-0-7636-3121-5

2 4 6 8 10 9 7 5 3 1

Printed in China

This book was typeset in Gararond and Fontesque.
The illustrations were done in ink and Adobe Photoshop®.

Candlewick Press
2067 Massachusetts Avenue
Cambridge, Massachussetts 02140

visit us at www.candlewick.com

THE FOURTH KING

CANDLEWICK PRESS
CAMBRIDGE, MASSACHUSETTS

TED SIEGER

ONCE UPON A TIME, THREE KINGS CAME OUT OF A DISTANT LAND and followed a star to a little town across the desert. You may know them as the Wise Men, or the Magi, or, as I did, by their names: Melchior, Caspar, and Balthazar. They brought with them gold, frankincense, and myrrh—presents for a newborn child.

But there was another king who set out on the long and difficult journey. Unlike the others, he arrived too late and empty-handed. I was that king, King Mazzel. I was the Fourth King.

I WAS THE RULER of a very small kingdom. It was so small that I was its king *and* its people! If it had not been for my camel, Chamberlin, I would have been all alone—except for the stars, my distant friends.

Like the Three Kings, I was a stargazer. Night after night I scoured the sky for the sign that would herald the birth of the King of Kings. Night after night I searched in vain. How long had I watched? A thousand nights? Ten thousand?

AND THEN one night it happened.

A bright star shone in the East. It was

the sign I had been waiting for!

My heart skipped a beat with joy.

In an instant we ran out the door, only

to run back in again.

After all, a king had been born—we

couldn't show up without a present!

I put on my royal cloak and packed

my most valuable possessions: the royal

star map and the royal star crystal.

We were on our way.

WE HAD TO HURRY. The Three Kings were waiting at the edge of the great desert, and the four of us would continue our journey together.

We rode through the night, leaving our home far behind, but I felt safe with the star as my guide. As the edge of the desert drew nearer, I looked forward to seeing my friends. But then the wind kicked up and stung our eyes with sand. The wind howled and bellowed, and the sandstorm started.

AFRAID FOR OUR LIVES, we plowed on through wave after wave of sand, hoping to outrun the storm and find shelter—but it seemed hopeless. And then, just as we were ready to drop in the dunes, we staggered out of the storm and into stillness.

It was Chamberlin who heard it first—a small cry on the wind. What were we to do? My friends were waiting, and we had such a long journey still ahead of us. What were we to do?

We headed back into the storm. And there, in its heart, we found a little nomad girl—sand-stung and frightened.

I wrapped her in my cloak and carried her through the blizzard.

We were glad to have found her and glad, too, when her family found us.
They invited us to stay, but I was anxious to join my friends.

We rode on, confident that we could make up the time. Yet when we
reached the desert's edge, the Three Kings had already left.

"MY DEAR MAZZEL," said the note. "We waited as long as we could. We have set off across the desert. One travels faster than three, and we are certain to see you before the journey's end. Your friend, Balthazar."

They weren't far ahead. We would surely catch up!

Chamberlin galloped faster than he had ever galloped in his life. But Chamberlin was quite a bit smaller than most camels, and his legs, though strong, weren't quite as long!

At last, I spied the Three Kings in the distance. . . .

ONLY IT WASN'T THEM. It was a merchant caravan—lost

and without a map. We weren't the only ones traveling that night.

Could I help them, perhaps?

But such a long camel train would travel very slowly, and according to my star

map, it was a long detour to their hometown. We were already late. What were we to do?

In slow procession, we led the caravan safely out of the desert. We would soon reach the

merchants' town.

I looked up, and my heart soared—I could still see the star! Perhaps we would

meet up with the Three Kings after all!

BUT THEN a deep gorge cut across our path.
There was no way around it. We would have
to cross over! The merchants were scared.
Their camels were scared. I was scared!
  But Chamberlin was with me,
and his courage
inspired us all.

AT THE OUTSKIRTS OF THEIR TOWN, we bade farewell to the merchants. So they wouldn't get lost again, we left the royal star map with the merchants and then set off.

The night was cool and silent, and the star glimmered like a candle in a faraway window. We rode until we were too weary to go on.

It was Chamberlin who heard it first—a tiny tinkling bell on the breeze. We looked around, but there was no one there. What were we to do? The tinkling came again.

but we did!

How we all made it I will never know . . .

Then I noticed
a small plant,
withered and
thirsty. I gave it
what little water
we had left.

To our amazement, the plant began to flower, then dropped a little round fruit that sounded like a bell into my palm.

We were astonished, and not a little puzzled. But the star was calling and I was anxious to join our friends, and so . . .

WE TRAVELED ON, following the star into the mountains.
The road grew steeper, and the wind grew icy. It started to rain,
and then the raindrops turned to hailstones. But Chamberlin
didn't seem to mind. I stayed close to him, afraid we would lose
sight of each other.

Finally we climbed above the clouds and found ourselves at the top of a mountain.

The star burned brightly. Full of hope once more, we tumbled after our friends.

WE SOON REACHED A VALLEY.
I felt sure we would catch up with
the Three Kings any moment.
But now we found our path blocked
by a strange, endless wall with
no gates or doorways.

There was no way through it;
we would have to go around it.
We hurried by as quickly as we could,
unsure of what was around the corner.

We were almost past when
we discovered the
terrible truth. . . .

The wall was being built
by small children.

THE CHILDREN WERE SLAVES belonging to a rich man who forced them to work on his wall. His guards seized us and carried us inside. I commanded the rich man to let the children go, but he just laughed.

I offered to give up my last gift for the newborn king in exchange for the children's freedom. The rich man snatched the crystal and said that it was ransom enough for my camel and me. We were free to go, but no one else.

What were we to do?

WE STAYED WITH THE CHILDREN and toiled with them to finish the wall. As we labored, the stones piled higher and hid the star from our view. And in spite of Chamberlin's best efforts to keep me from despair, my hopes were fading fast.

Seeing my sadness, a little girl gave me her only possession—a toy lamb carved from wood. It made me smile. I hid the lamb in my tunic and promised her that, somehow, we would all be free.

BUT NOT YET. Instead, the guards herded us all into a dark stone maze. We could hardly see each other in the blackness, so the children huddled close to me and Chamberlin. How would we ever escape?

It was Chamberlin who heard it first — a tiny tinkling bell. The fruit from the desert.

It cracked open in my hand to reveal three softly luminous star-seeds. Their light shone in the darkness as Chamberlin led us out through the maze, then, on tiptoes, past the sleeping guards and out of our prison. We lifted the children through the last small opening in the wall. We were free!

THE CHILDREN CAME WITH US. I felt sure they would be safe with the newborn king.

The star led us on toward a little town called Bethlehem. There we met some shepherds with glad tidings. They had followed the star to a stable at the edge of town, where they had visited a baby and seen the Three Kings. My heart sang with joy!

But the shepherds stopped us. Something terrible was happening in Bethlehem. Soldiers sent to kill the King of Kings were killing all the small children in the town. I thought of that tiny baby, born in a stable— I had to save him!

WE LEFT THE CHILDREN WITH THE SHEPHERDS and raced down the hillside, but soldiers were searching the valley, so we hid among the ruins until they had passed. Then out of the shadows, a man appeared, leading a donkey; seated atop the donkey was a woman with a baby in her arms. They looked frightened, and the baby was starting to stir, so I beckoned them to our hiding place—not a moment too soon.

We sat silently as the soldiers passed by—except for the newborn child, who started to whimper. Quickly, I gave him the wooden lamb from my pocket, and he beamed with hushed delight.

But the soldiers had turned back and were coming closer. What were we to do? They were sure to discover us. What were we to do?

There was only one thing to do. With a deep breath, I leaped out onto the road, Chamberlin at my side, and ran, hoping that we could distract the soldiers long enough for the family to make their escape.

Sure enough, the soldiers gave chase and were soon gaining on us. Somehow, we drew our pursuers into the next valley before I stumbled to a stop, exhausted. Chamberlin stood guard as the troops closed in, their swords drawn menacingly. We were outnumbered and, it seemed, out of luck. . . .

To this day, I don't know what happened next. The earth shook, and our ears were full of thunder. And the soldiers? They were much afraid and fled in confusion. I cannot be certain, but I like to think that they had been scattered by the stampeding of three royal camels.

Chamberlin and I were alone on the edge of town. The stable that the shepherds had spoken about was up ahead. We ran as fast as we could, but the stable was empty. We were too late! Our journey had been in vain. I fell to my knees and wept.

AND THEN, IN THE DEPTHS
OF MY DESPAIR, the most wonderful
thing happened. I heard a voice
speak softly.

"King Mazzel, you have not come too late!
You were always with me.
When I was lost, you showed me the way.
When I was thirsty, you gave me water.
When I was captive, you freed me.
When I was in danger, you saved me.
You were always there
when I needed you,
and I will be with you forever."

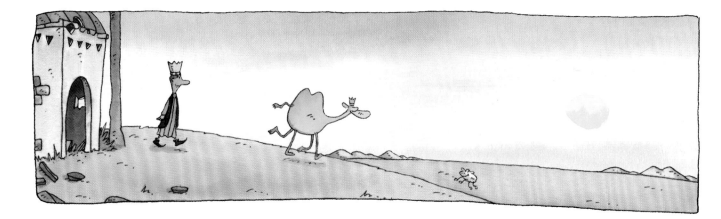

HEARING THESE WORDS, I knew that my journey was over. My heart was filled with joy. The rising sun felt warm on my face. A new day was dawning.

Outside the stable, the shepherds and the children were waiting. Full of smiles, we embraced and set off into the countryside.

And so, though it hardly matters now, I never did meet the Three Kings.
Balthazar, Caspar, and Melchior returned to their kingdoms, but I did not.

I am no longer a king. I am a shepherd, and Chamberlin is a sheep camel.
He looks after our sheep, and I look after our flock of children. We are very happy.

From time to time we still like to walk in the meadow and watch the night sky.
And though the star has long disappeared from its place,
it still burns brightly in my heart.